AMULET

Library of Congress Control Number: 2017955789

ISBN 978-0-545-85002-5 (hardcover)
ISBN 978-0-545-82860-4 (paperback)

10 9 8 7 6 5 4 3 2   18 19 20 21 22

Printed in China   62
First edition, October 2018
Edited by Cassandra Pelham Fulton
Book design by Kazu Kibuishi and Phil Falco
Creative Director: David Saylor

AMULET

KAZU KIBUISHI

BOOK EIGHT
SUPERNOVA

AN IMPRINT OF
SCHOLASTIC

4

TRELLIS, THE ELF ARMY HAS MADE LANDFALL.

BALAN AND I HAVE PREPARED A TRIAGE CENTER TO CARE FOR THE WOUNDED.

UNFORTUNATELY, WE ARE SHORT ON MEDICAL STAFF.

THEN LET'S HOPE WE WON'T NEED ANY.

HE IS AN ELF, AFTER ALL.

SO AM I, DOC.

PRINCE TRELLIS WILL FACE THEM.

WE SHALL SEE HOW HE INTENDS TO DIFFUSE THE SITUATION.

CAN WE TRUST HIM?

OH, RIGHT!

BUT YOU'RE NOT RELATED TO THE ELF KING!

NO.

HOWEVER, MY FAMILY HAD QUITE A FEW TRAITS THAT I HOPE I DID NOT INHERIT.

WELL, I SUPPOSE WE CAN USE ALL THE HELP WE CAN GET!

HEY DOC, SPEAKING OF HELP, LET'S ROUND UP SOME MORE VOLUNTEERS.

RIVA!

10

RIVA, WE SEE SOLDIERS LEAVING THEIR POSTS.

THEY ARE CONCERNED.

CONCERNED?

BUT WE HAVE FORCES ON THE GROUND TO MEET THE ELF ARMY.

YOU ONLY NEED TO PROTECT WHAT'S INSIDE THE WALLS!

IT'S NOT THAT, RIVA.

IT'S OUR FAMILIES.

THE COUNCIL HAS ORDERED ALL CHILDREN AND THEIR MOTHERS BE EVACUATED.

WE WANT TO GO WITH THEM.

THEY'RE USING THE CHARNON HOUSE.

PATRICK, STOP THEM FROM LEAVING THE CITY.

GOT IT.

WE WILL SEE TO IT THAT YOUR FAMILIES STAY HERE AND REMAIN SAFE.

THANK YOU.

THEN WE NEED TO GET WEAPONS!

NO! WE LET THE STONEKEEPERS TAKE CARE OF THE THREAT--

WHILE WE FOCUS ON KEEPING THE CITY CALM.

THAT'S WHAT WE'RE TRYING TO DO!

PATRICK! WHAT IS GOING ON OUT THERE? THE SOLDIERS WANT US TO EVACUATE!

THE ELF ARMY IS ON THEIR WAY!

BUT ALL THE FAMILIES ARE LOOKING TO GET OUT OF HERE!

IT'S A MAD-HOUSE!

PATRICK, WHERE ARE YOU GOING?!

TO CONVINCE THEM THAT THEY ARE SAFER IN THE CITY!

EXCUSE ME! PARDON ME!

COMING THROUGH!

LET US IN, YOU MONSTER!

AT LEAST LET THE CHILDREN THROUGH!

STOP PUSHING!

EVERYONE PLEASE STAY CALM!

THE HOUSE IS TOO FULL, BUT WE WILL FIND A WAY TO GET EVERYONE ON BOARD!

LIAR!

MORRIE! TELL EVERYONE TO RETURN TO THEIR HOMES!

WE'RE NOT GOING ANYWHERE, KID!

I WAS TOLD TO BRING ABOARD ALL WOMEN AND CHILDREN!

BUT THEY CAN'T ALL FIT IN THE CHARNON HOUSE, AND IT'S JUST CAUSING THEM TO PANIC.

EVERYONE NEEDS TO GO BACK TO THEIR HOMES.

EASIER SAID THAN DONE, PATRICK!

WE HAVE A LOT OF PASSENGERS ON BOARD!

YOU'RE RIGHT.

THIS MIGHT TAKE A WHILE.

WE CAN ACCOMMODATE MAYBE THIRTY SOLDIERS IN HERE AT MOST.

I KNOW. I KNOW. IT'S SMALL.

BUT IT'S WHAT WE HAVE.

ON THE BRIGHT SIDE, THE DOCTORS AND NURSES IN IPPO HAVE BEEN AMAZING.

YOU'RE RIGHT. WE OWE THE CITIZENS HERE A GREAT DEBT OF GRATITUDE.

THIS IS SOMETHING I WILL NOT FORGET.

AHEM--

WHAT IS IT, BOGEN?

MESSAGE FOR MISS RIVA.

MISTER LIGHT WOULD LIKE TO SPEAK WITH YOU.

A GREAT SEA CHANGE IS ABOUT TO OCCUR.

THIS WAR SIGNALS THE END OF THE ELF ARMY AS WE KNOW IT.

A NEW ONE IS ABOUT TO TAKE ITS PLACE.

AND THEY WILL REQUIRE LEADERS.

LEADERS LIKE YOU.

I AM A PART OF THE RESISTANCE.

WHY WOULD I WANT TO HELP LEAD THE ELF ARMY?

THEY SEE ME AS THEIR ENEMY.

THEY ARE STILL YOUR PEOPLE.

MY FOCUS IS ON HELPING THE RESISTANCE TAKE DOWN THE ELF KING.

THAT'S IT. THAT'S MY MISSION.

MAY I SUGGEST LOOKING FURTHER AHEAD?

LOOK PAST WHAT YOU SEE IN FRONT OF YOU.

THE ELVES WILL HAVE NEW LEADERS SOON.

TRELLIS?

YOU'RE TALKING ABOUT PRINCE TRELLIS.

TRELLIS CAN'T LEAD THEM ON HIS OWN.

HE WILL TRY, BUT THE RESPONSIBILITIES WILL BE OVERWHELMING.

HE'S GOING TO NEED OUR HELP.

LOGI.

HUF HUF HUF

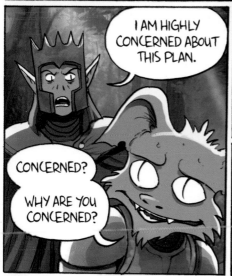

I AM HIGHLY CONCERNED ABOUT THIS PLAN.

OUR FORCES ARE DEPLETED.

OUR TROOPS ARE NOT PREPARED TO BATTLE THE IPPO ARMY AND THE RESISTANCE.

CONCERNED?

WHY ARE YOU CONCERNED?

YES.

BOTH VALID CONCERNS.

AND BOTH VERY TRUE.

THEN WHY ARE WE DOING THIS?!

BECAUSE IT IS NOT OUR DUTY TO THINK, SERGEANT.

IT IS OUR DUTY TO FOLLOW THE KING'S ORDERS.

OUR KING HAS A GLORIOUS PLAN FOR US AND WE MUST CARRY IT OUT.

DO YOU NOT TRUST YOUR KING?

MY LOYALTY TO THE KING HAS NEVER WAVERED! NOT ONCE!

I SIMPLY DON'T SEE HOW THIS PLAN OF ATTACK IS GOING TO WORK!

IF WE WALK RIGHT UP TO THEIR FRONT DOOR, WE WILL GET DESTROYED.

IS THIS NOT APPARENT?

WE WILL LOSE THIS FIGHT!

THE KING DOES NOT COMMAND US TO FIGHT.

HIS ORDERS ARE FOR US TO TURN OURSELVES IN.

WHAT?!

DIRECT ORDERS FROM THE KING HIMSELF.

NO FIGHTING. NO SHOW OF FORCE. WE ARE TO SIMPLY SURRENDER.

NO! THIS IS NOT POSSIBLE!

DID YOU ALL COME HERE JUST TO GIVE UP?!

WE ARE TIRED AND HUNGRY, BROTHER.

IT'S BETTER THIS WAY.

THE KING IS MAKING A MISTAKE.

YOU WILL JOIN US.

IF YOU KNOW WHAT'S BEST FOR YOU.

NO.

SOMETHING'S NOT RIGHT.

WE NEED TO ATTACK NOW.

SH.

HM?

PRINCE TRELLIS,

IS THAT YOU?

OUR MEN DO NOT HAVE ENOUGH FOOD TO EAT OR HOMES TO DEFEND.

WE ARE HERE TO SURRENDER!

PLEASE ACCEPT OUR SURRENDER AS A GIFT FROM YOUR LOYAL SERVANT, LOGI!

I BELIEVE WE WILL BE BETTER SERVED AS YOUR PRISONERS THAN AS YOUR FATHER'S SOLDIERS.

CAN WE TRUST HIM?

NO.

LOGI HAS ALWAYS BEEN LOYAL TO MY FATHER.

HE'S UP TO SOMETHING.

BUT THOSE SOLDIERS DO NOT KNOW THAT.

AND WE CAN'T SIMPLY ATTACK THEM.

JUST LET ME HANDLE THIS.

WHERE ARE YOU GOING?!

TRELLIS!

EVERYBODY, WEAPONS DOWN!

WE ARE NO MATCH FOR A STONEKEEPER!

PUT YOUR WEAPONS DOWN!

KLAK!

KLAK!

THE TROOPS ARE NOW YOURS TO COMMAND.

HEY! TAKE IT EASY!

YOU'RE LUCKY TO BE ALIVE, ELF! NO COMPLAINING!

WHAT ARE YOU UP TO, LOGI?

WHAT DO YOU MEAN?

YOU WERE ALWAYS FIERCELY LOYAL TO MY FATHER.

MY DUTY HAS ALWAYS BEEN TO SERVE THE ELF ARMY FIRST.

NOT JUST THE KING.

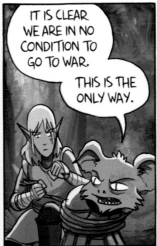

IT IS CLEAR WE ARE IN NO CONDITION TO GO TO WAR.

THIS IS THE ONLY WAY.

THE WAR IS A FIGHT BETWEEN STONE-KEEPERS, AFTER ALL.

THE REST OF US ARE SIMPLY PAWNS IN YOUR GAME.

THAT WAS PROBABLY THE EASIEST BATTLE I'VE BEEN A PART OF, MATE.

ALL THANKS TO YOU!

THESE ELVES ARE NOT THE REAL ENEMY, CAPTAIN.

WE HAVE A FIGHT AHEAD OF US.

HAH! I RECOMMEND LOOSENING UP A LITTLE!

WE HAVE TO ENJOY THE SMALL VICTORIES, MATE.

ESPECIALLY WHEN THE GOOD TIMES TEND TO BE FLEETING.

THEY'RE BACK!

OPEN THE GATES!

THE ELF ARMY HAS SURRENDERED!

HM.

THE ELF PRINCE REALLY DID IT.

HE SAVED US!

SURRENDERED?

LET THE WARDEN KNOW TO PREPARE FOR A LARGE INFLUX OF PRISONERS.

YES, COMMANDER.

TRELLIS-- WHAT HAPPENED OUT THERE?

LOGI TURNED HIMSELF IN.

THIS IS VERY STRANGE.

LOGI WOULD NEVER ACT ON HIS OWN, AGAINST MY FATHER'S WISHES.

HE WOULD DO ANYTHING FOR MY FAMILY.

HE MUST STILL BE FOLLOWING ORDERS.

YOU THINK IT'S A TRAP?

WE JUST NEED TO STAY ON ALERT.

THERE YOU ARE, RIVA!

TONIGHT WE WILL LIGHT UP THE SKY WITH FIREWORKS!

WE WILL SERVE OUR VERY BEST FOOD IN A GREAT FEAST!

AND YOU WILL BE OUR GUESTS OF HONOR!

WE REALLY CAN'T TAKE THE TIME TO--

AHEM, YOUR MAJESTY.

THEY HAVE DONE SO MUCH FOR US.

ATTENDING A DINNER IN YOUR HONOR IS THE LEAST YOU COULD DO.

I WILL ACCEPT.

SPLENDID!

THIS WILL BE A CELEBRATION THAT YOU WILL NOT FORGET!

RELAX.

GO ATTEND THE BANQUET, AND LET ME WORRY ABOUT LOGI.

I HARDLY DID ANYTHING TO HELP THESE PEOPLE. THIS WAR IS FAR FROM OVER.

DON'T BE SO HARD ON YOURSELF, PRINCE TRELLIS.

WHEN THIS WAR COMES TO AN END, THE NEXT ONE WON'T BE FAR BEHIND.

YOU'RE OLD ENOUGH TO KNOW THIS IS HOW IT'S ALWAYS BEEN.

YOU DON'T UNDERSTAND WHAT WE'RE UP AGAINST. THE VOICE HAS EMILY UNDER HIS CONTROL.

THE VOICE?

HE'S THE ONE INSTIGATING THIS WAR. AND HE PLANS TO USE EMILY AND HER POWERS TO DESTROY US ALL.

THIS CONFLICT WAS NEVER ABOUT THE ELVES OR ABOUT MY FAMILY.

HE USED US TO SPREAD CHAOS AND DISORDER.

WHY WOULD THE VOICE DO ALL THIS?

TO MAKE THE PEOPLE OF ALLEDIA VULNERABLE.

TO MAKE US WEAK.

HE'S PREPARING OUR PLANET FOR THE ARRIVAL OF HIS MASTERS.

AND WHO ARE HIS MASTERS?

I THINK WE'RE ABOUT TO FIND OUT.

HEY, RICO!

WHAT ARE YOU DOING?!

HOW COME WE DON'T GET TO JOIN THE PARTY?

PARTY?!

WE DON'T HAVE TIME TO PARTY!

WE'RE SUPPOSED TO BE WATCHING OVER THE CITY!

NOW HELP US TIE SOME KNOTS!

SIGH.

AH!

MASTER VIGO!

I AM HONORED THAT YOU HAVE COME TO VISIT OLD LOGI!

LET'S CUT THE SMALL TALK.

WHY ARE YOU HERE?

IT IS LIKE I SAID!

I DID THIS FOR OUR TROOPS.

I DID IT WITH THEIR BEST INTERESTS IN MIND.

THE PRISON'S BEING ATTACKED.

VIGO!

TELL THE CITIZENS TO FIND A BUNKER OR A BASEMENT!

YES, CALM!

BUT KEEP EVERYONE CALM!

AND WHERE IS PRINCE TRELLIS GOING?

TRELLIS?

MAYOR RIVA!

PLEASE GUIDE ME THROUGH THIS!

TRELLIS!

HWEEEEEEE

BOOM!!

CRASH!!

ARE YOU ALL RIGHT?

YOU NEED TO GET OUT OF HERE.

YOU ARE BOTH IN TERRIBLE DANGER, SO YOU MUST LEAVE NOW!

WHERE DO WE GO?

THIS IS OUR HOME.

PACK FOOD AND WATER.

GO TO THE TOWN SQUARE.

WHEREVER YOU DECIDE TO GO, JUST LEAVE THIS HOUSE.

IT IS NOT SAFE HERE!

LEAVE, NOW!

52

FWOOMP!

AH!

JOS, GO! JUST GO!

DAD!

I CAN PULL YOU OUT!

DAD! JUST--

GIVE ME YOUR HAND!

NGH!

VIGO! HOW DID YOU CHASE AWAY THE PHOENIX?

EMILY STOPPED THE PHOENIX HERSELF. SHE STILL RETAINS SOME CONTROL.

I DIDN'T.

WE NEED TO GO FIND HER IN THE VOID.

NO.

WE AGREED THAT IF SOMETHING WENT WRONG, WE MEET IN CIELIS.

THAT'S WHERE EMILY WILL BE HEADED IF SHE MANAGES TO RECOVER.

SO WE MUST MOVE FORWARD WITH THE BELIEF THAT SHE WILL JOIN US THERE.

HER FATE IS IN HER OWN HANDS NOW.

LEON? HAVE YOU BEEN AWAKE ALL THIS TIME?

OH.

IT'S BEEN HARD TO SLEEP.

I'M HAVING DIFFICULTY SLEEPING, TOO. CAN I JOIN YOU?

YES. OF COURSE. I MADE TEA.

PLEASE HAVE SOME.

SSSIP...

WE'RE IN SPACE.

YES.

LIFE IS FULL OF UNEXPECTED ADVENTURES.

SSIP.

I'M HERE BECAUSE I THOUGHT I COULD HELP THE PEOPLE OF ALLEDIA.

AND NOW, I FEEL LIKE I FAILED.

YOU MUST SENSE IT, TOO.

EMILY IS IN TROUBLE.

SOMETHING IS DEFINITELY WRONG.

I DO FEEL IT.

BUT WHAT CAN WE DO FROM HERE?

HOPE.

WE HOPE THAT YOUR DAUGHTER IS AS STRONG AS WE THINK SHE IS.

AND WE FOCUS ON HELPING NAVIN.

WE PROVIDE HIM WITH GUIDANCE AND TOOLS HE NEEDS TO BE A LEADER.

RISE AND SHINE, PILOTS.

WE'RE PREPARING TO DOCK.

MOM?

YOU OKAY?

YES. SNIFF. I'M FINE. I'M FINE.

THIS IS OUR DESTINATION, LIGHTHOUSE ONE.

IT SERVES AS THE BASE OF OPERATIONS FOR THE RESISTANCE.

YOU'RE GOING TO DRIVE ONE OF THOSE?

I'M PRETTY SURE THAT'S WHY WE'RE HERE.

THESE COLOSSUS SUITS LOOK A LOT MORE ADVANCED THAN THE ONES ON ALLEDIA.

THIS SHOULD BE INTERESTING.

MORE ALLEDIANS, RIGHT?

YEP.

THEY'RE WILLING TO WORK WITH US, SO BE NICE.

GOOD GRIEF.

HELLO, MY FRIENDS!

WELCOME TO LIGHTHOUSE ONE!

WE ARE SO GLAD TO HAVE YOU HERE!

YES!

PLEASE FOLLOW US!

THEY SEEM VERY NICE.

WE'LL NEED TO MAKE SURE YOU'RE ALL CLEAR OF VIRUSES OR BACTERIA.

TWENTY MINUTES IN THE UV CHAMBER SHOULD DO IT.

EVERYBODY, WATCH YOUR STEP.

I LIKE TO CALL THIS THE SPACE SAUNA!

WELCOME ABOARD!

IRRADIATION SEQUENCE INITIATING.

PST!

PHOO.

I NEED TO TALK WITH ENGINEERING ABOUT PUTTING FANS IN THESE SUITS.

I'M DRENCHED IN SWEAT!

GOOD LUCK WITH THAT, BUDDY!

HM.

MINT?

YOU CAN RELAX. WE'LL BE IN HERE FOR A WHILE.

MY NAME'S BENTO, BY THE WAY.

MY FRIEND'S NAME IS FLON.

OH, I'M NAVIN. NAVIN HAYES.

I HOPE YOU DON'T MIND MY ASKING --

BUT WHERE ARE YOU GUYS FROM?

I'M FROM DOONYA, A SMALL TOWN WEST OF THE FLAMING SEA.

FLON'S FROM THE METAL CITY, KODORA.

THE FACT OF THE MATTER IS THAT WE'RE ALL FROM SOME-PLACE ELSE.

OUR HOME PLANETS ARE MANY STARS APART,

BUT BEN TO AND I HAVE BEEN FRIENDS FOR YEARS!

WHAT BROUGHT YOU TWO TOGETHER?

BOTH OF OUR PLANETS HAVE BEEN OVERRUN BY SHADOW CREATURES.

OUR PEOPLE ARE SUFFERING.

WE TRACKED THE SOURCE OF THE SHADOWS, AND THEY COME FROM THE PLANET BELOW US.

WE'RE HERE TO SEE IF WE CAN STOP THEM.

SO, YOU GUYS ARE PILOTS?

NO. YOU'RE THE PILOTS.

WE'RE THE MEDICS.

YOU'LL BE JOINING US AS PART OF THE CREW OF OUR S.A.M. UNIT.

WHAT'S A SAM UNIT?

S.A.M. IS AN ACRONYM FOR SUPPORT ASSIST MECH.

OUR UNIT CONSISTS OF A TEAM OF SCIENTISTS, MECHANICS, SOLDIERS, AND MEDICS TRAINED TO HELP OTHER UNITS ON THE FIELD.

WE'RE THE ONES WHO HELP THE HELPERS!

DETOXIFICATION COMPLETE!

WELCOME ABOARD!

EVERYONE STAY ALERT.

GOOD PILOTS HAVE BEEN VERY DIFFICULT TO FIND OR TRAIN--

JAIDOH, I'D LIKE TO INTRO--

HEY!

WHO BROUGHT THE ROBOTS?

ARE THEY SECURE?

SECURE?

WHAT ARE YOU TALKING ABOUT, MA'AM?!

YOU FELLAS ARE VULNERABLE TO POTENTIAL HACKS.

IMPOSSIBLE!

YOU SOUND QUITE SURE OF YOURSELF.

BEEP

BEEP

MY OPERATING SYSTEM IS THE BEST YOU--

ERK!

BZT!!

BEEP BEEP BEEP

AGH!

BEEP BEEP BEEP

ERGH!

WHY CAN'T I STOP THE DANCING?!

MAKE IT STOP!!

AS YOU CAN SEE, I WAS ABLE TO HACK INTO YOUR SYSTEM.

YOU NEED NEW SOFTWARE.

I CAN HELP WITH THAT.

UNGH...

WOW.

THE ROBOT KNOWN AS MISKIT.

YOU, ON THE OTHER HAND, ARE A DIFFERENT STORY.

WHO WROTE THIS PROGRAM?

SILAS CHARNON.

OH.

WELL, THAT FIGURES.

NOT EVERY DAY YOU GET TO SEE THE WORK OF A FAMOUS GUY.

I'LL ADMIT, THOUGH--

HE KNEW HIS STUFF.

I DIDN'T REALIZE ROBOTS COULD BE TAKEN OVER LIKE THAT.

IT'S NOT JUST ROBOTS, KID. YOU'VE SEEN THE SHADOWS?

THOSE THINGS CAN TAKE OVER ANY LIVING THING!

IN FACT, ROBOTS ARE JUST ABOUT THE ONLY THINGS THAT ARE IMMUNE.

I'M TERRIBLY EMBARRASSED.

I PROMISE IT WILL NOT OCCUR AGAIN.

WHAT HAPPENS IF SOMEONE TAKEN OVER BY SHADOWS TAKES OVER A ROBOT?

NOW YOU'RE ASKING THE QUESTIONS THAT KEEP ME UP AT NIGHT.

WE JUST HAVE TO WORK TO STAY AHEAD OF THEM.

WELCOME TO LIFE IN INTERESTING TIMES, KID!

NOW LET ME SHOW YOU AROUND THE GIANT ROBOT YOU'RE GOING TO COMMAND.

THE CONTROLS LOOK A LOT LIKE A SILVERHAWK'S.

EXCEPT THEY HAVE SCREENS ON THEM.

HELLO.

THAT IS CODY.

SHORT FOR CO-DRIVER.

HE CAN HELP BY SUGGESTING ACTIONS AND DIRECTIONS.

IS HE THE AUTO-PILOT?

HE IS WHAT YOU NEED HIM TO BE.

HE CAN PILOT S.A.M. IF YOU NEED HIM TO.

PERSONALLY, I WOULD PREFER THAT YOU ALWAYS MAINTAIN THE CONTROLS.

CODY KNOWS I DON'T FULLY TRUST HIM--

BUT I WILL NOT DENY HIS USEFULNESS.

I APPRECIATE THAT, JAIDOH.

WHEN WE'RE ON OUR MISSION, WE WILL NEED RESILIENT GEAR AND TOOLS.

THAT'S WHY WE'VE ASSIGNED A TEAM OF LLORTS TO TEST ALL OUR EQUIPMENT.

CRAK!

IS HE TRYING TO BREAK THAT BIKE?

YES.

IF A LLORT CAN BREAK SOMETHING, THEN WE SEND IT BACK TO THE LAB.

IF THE EQUIPMENT HOLDS UP IN TESTING, WE CONSIDER IT FOR USE ON MISSIONS.

LOOKS LIKE THE BIKES ARE HOLDING UP.

WHACK!!

THE LAST THING YOU WANT IS TO FIND OUT YOUR EQUIPMENT DOESN'T HOLD UP OUT ON THE FIELD.

WE'LL MAKE SURE YOU'RE PROPERLY GEARED UP!

THESE FEEL COMFORTABLE.

GOOD.

WE WILL PAIR THEM WITH LESS EXPENSIVE SOCKS TO FIT THEM IN THE BUDGET.

SHIRTS, PANTS, AND UNDERGARMENTS ARE SIMPLE BUT STRONG.

NOTHING FANCY, SO WE CAN SAVE ON COST HERE.

HOWEVER, THE OUTERWEAR SEES SIGNIFICANT USE.

WE INVEST IN THAT.

WE HAVE WORKED WITH CRAFTSMEN ON GHEN-7 TO CREATE VERY LIGHT AND STRONG ARMOR.

THESE HELMETS ARE MADE FROM THE SILK OF A PROTECK SANDWORM.

THEY'RE SO LIGHT!

THIS IS YOUR SUPPLY PACK.

IT CONTAINS PRESERVED FOOD, TOOLS, AND BOOKS.

I KNOW WHAT YOU'RE GOING TO FACE OUT THERE.

I HOPE THAT YOUR TEACHERS HAVE TAUGHT YOU WELL.

LEON REDBEARD. MY CREW SCAN TELLS ME YOU ARE NOT A FOX, SO I MUST BE MISSING SOME INFORMATION.

CARE TO EXPLAIN?

YOU ARE ASKING ABOUT MY APPEARANCE.

THIS IS A CURSE. MANY PEOPLE ON ALLEDIA HAVE BEEN AFFECTED BY IT.

YOU'RE HERE TO FIND A CURE?

NO.

I MADE PEACE WITH THIS CURSE LONG AGO.

THEN WHAT BRINGS YOU ALL THE WAY OUT HERE?

I AM HERE TO HELP THOSE WHO BELIEVE IN THE VIRTUES OF PEACE.

PEACE? BUT YOU'RE A FIGHTER.

I WILL FIGHT FOR PEACE.

GLAD TO HAVE YOU ON THIS CREW, LEON REDBEARD.

ALL SUPPORT ASSIST MECH CREWS REPORT TO VESSELS.

S.A.M. THREE, S.A.M. FOUR, S.A.M. FIVE, PREPARE FOR DEPLOYMENT TO TYPHON BASE.

CODY, START WARM-UP SEQUENCE FOR THE CENTRAL BOOSTERS.

WE DO NOT HAVE ANY CENTRAL BOOSTERS.

WHAT?

THEN HOW DO WE FLY?

USING JUST THE SECONDARY BOOSTERS.

I HAD THE CENTRAL ONES REMOVED FOR MANEUVERABILITY.

YOU WILL THANK ME LATER.

GET US TO TYPHON, CODY.

S.A.M. FOUR DEPLOYED.

S.A.M. FIVE READY FOR DEPLOYMENT.

YES, JAIDOH. PLANNING ROUTES NOW.

AFTER LIFTING INTO ZERO GRAVITY, ADJUST S.A.M.'S POSITION ANGLE TOWARD TYPHON BASE SEVEN.

JUST ONE GOOD BLAST FROM THE SECONDARY BOOSTERS SHOULD GIVE US THE FORCE WE NEED.

YOU WILL GET USED TO BEING THE SMALL FRY.

S.A.M.S ARE DESIGNED FOR MOBILITY, NOT STRENGTH.

EVERYTHING HERE IS JUST SO BIG.

WE'RE HERE TO BRING PEOPLE WHAT THEY NEED.

REPAIR AND PROVIDE AID WHEN POSSIBLE.

OUR FIRST REQUESTS ARE COMING IN NOW.

WE CAN BEGIN ASSISTING ON THE FIELD.

JAIDOH, WHAT IS THAT?

THAT IS A MINEROC IN NEED OF MEDICAL ATTENTION--

OUR FIRST ASSIGNMENT OF THE DAY.

S.A.M. FIVE, CAN YOU PROVIDE US WITH AN INTERNAL SCAN?

WE CAN CERTAINLY ACCOMMODATE. BENTO, SEND OUT SCOUTS.

KSSHT!

VNNN!

VNNNNNNNNN...

VNNNNNN.

VNNNNN!

A JOURNEY DOWN THE OLD SNOT CAVES.

THIS MIGHT TAKE A WHILE.

TYPHON BASE HAS AN URGENT REQUEST FOR OUR CREW.

THEY NEED TO REACH A GADOBA TREE FARM AND RETRIEVE SAPLINGS.

THE FARM IS LOCATED AT THE TOP OF MOUNT SUGINO, A FIFTY-MILE JOURNEY.

WE CAN FLY UP AFTER OUR JOB HERE IS DONE.

NEGATIVE.

WE CAN'T RISK LOSING S.A.M. FIVE TO AN E.M.P. BLAST.

NO MOTORIZED, ELECTRIC VEHICLES CAN ACCESS THE TREE FARM.

HEY, WAIT--

WE HAVE BIKES.

133

VRRRRRNNN

KSSH!!!

SO YOUNG TO BE PILOTS WHO WORK WITH DOCTORS.

ON ALLEDIA, GADOBA TREES BEAR FRUIT THAT HAVE THE ABILTY TO GIVE AND TAKE LIFE.

I SEE NO FRUITS, SO MAY I ASK WHAT GROWS FROM YOUR BRANCHES?

OUR FEATHERED BRANCHES CLEAN THE ATMOSPHERE OF TYPHON.

WE DO OUR PART TO MAKE THIS WORLD A PLACE WHERE WE CAN COEXIST IN RELATIVE PEACE.

WHAT DO YOU MEAN WHEN YOU SAY "RELATIVE PEACE"?

WE TRY TO KEEP THE CHILDREN OF THIS PLANET FROM FIGHTING, OF COURSE.

MOST TIMES WE CANNOT STEM THE TIDE OF CONFLICT. BUT WE DO TRY.

IN THE MEANTIME, PLEASE FIND A GOOD HOME FOR OUR LITTLE BROTHERS.

WE PROMISE TO TAKE GREAT CARE OF THEM.

THANK YOU.

JAIDOH, WE MADE IT TO THE FARM AND WE HAVE THE SAPLINGS.

GOOD WORK!

HOWEVER, YOU ARE LOSING SUNLIGHT.

I SUGGEST STAYING THE NIGHT BEFORE HEADING BACK TO BASE.

YOU'RE BOTH VERY WELCOME TO STAY WITH US.

MAMA WILL BE THRILLED.

THANK YOU, LUCY.

I'M FROM THE CITY OF CIELIS ON ALLEDIA.

NAVIN IS FROM THE PLANET EARTH.

HAVE THE SHADOWS CAUSED PROBLEMS ON YOUR PLANETS?

YES. MANY OF OUR CITIES ARE UNDER SIEGE FROM THE SHADOWS.

MY SISTER FOUND ONE ON EARTH.

WHEN YOU SEE ONE, YOU CAN BE SURE THERE ARE MANY MORE OF THEM.

PRETTY SOON, THE PLANET WILL BE OVERRUN BY SHADOWS.

YOU SAID YOU HAVE A SISTER.

WHAT'S HER NAME?

EMILY.

WHERE IS EMILY NOW?

SHE'S STILL ON ALLEDIA.

WORKING TO RESTORE THE GUARDIAN COUNCIL.

YOUR SISTER IS A STONEKEEPER?

DO YOU KNOW WHAT HAPPENS WHEN THEY LOSE CONTROL OF THEIR POWERS?

ARE YOU A GOOD LEADER?

PEOPLE ARE ALWAYS CALLING HIM COMMANDER FOR SOME REASON.

I'M NOT TRYING TO BE A LEADER.

I JUST WANT TO HELP.

GOOD!

YOU CAN BEGIN BY TAKING THESE SAPLINGS TO BASE IN THE MORNING.

PLEASE REMEMBER THAT THESE TREES ARE FAMILY TO US.

AND NOW YOU ARE BOTH A PART OF OUR FAMILY AS WELL.

WHOOOOSHH!!

SO MUCH WIND.

HEY, HAYES, I'VE GOT SOMETHING TO TELL YOU.

YEAH?

YOU'RE A GOOD PERSON, AND I APPRECIATE THAT.

I DON'T THINK I EVER SAID IT TO YOU BEFORE.

THANKS, ALY.

KEEP UP THE GOOD WORK, HAYES.

OKAY.

ONE THING, THOUGH.

CAN YOU STOP CALLING ME HAYES?

SURE THING, PAL.

HEHEH.

GOOD NIGHT, ALY.

GOOD NIGHT, NAVIN.

WHOOOOOSH!!

WHOOOSH!!

WAKE UP, COMMANDER!

HUH?

BOOM!

YOU AND ALY NEED TO GET DOWN THE MOUNTAIN NOW!

KOOM! BOOM!

EVERYBODY HOLD ON!

JAIDOH, WHAT IS GOING ON?

I'LL EXPLAIN LATER.

I SEE ON THE MAP THAT YOU HAVE A PATH DOWN THE EAST SIDE OF THE MOUNTAIN.

TAKE THAT PATH AND MEET US AT THE BOTTOM.

GO, NOW.

DID YOU SEE THE EXPLOSIONS BEHIND JAIDOH?

SOMETHING'S WRONG.

HUF HUF HUF HUF.

GOOD MORNING, PILOTS!

WEATHER'S A BIT ROUGH FOR A RIDE TODAY.

THIS IS THE FASTEST WAY DOWN.

IT'S ALSO THE MOST DIFFICULT TRAIL.

IS THAT A TORNADO?

BOOM!

IT'S A SHADOW STORM.

THAT MEANS THE STONE GIANTS ARE ON THE MOVE.

YOU NEED TO BE CAREFUL.

BEEP BEEP WHIRRRR

KSHT!

THE TREE SAPLINGS ARE SAFELY SECURED IN YOUR PACKS.

PLEASE TAKE CARE OF THEM.

WE WILL.

I'M VERY GLAD TO HAVE MET YOU AND ALY.

I HOPE OUR PATHS CROSS AGAIN!

I HOPE SO, TOO!

LET'S GO, NAVIN!

FOLLOW ME!

THIS IS SO STEEP.

IT'S ALL ABOUT CHOOSING A GOOD LINE AND TRUSTING YOUR SKILLS.

STAY FOCUSED.

STAY RELAXED.

WOO HOO!

AND TRY TO HAVE FUN.

WHOOO. OKAY.

RRT!

WHOA. WHOA. WHOA!

RRT! SKSH!

JAIDOH, WHAT IS GOING ON OVER THERE?!

TYPHON BASE IS GONE.

MOST OF OUR MECHS ARE DESTROYED.

WE ARE PART OF ONLY A SMALL HANDFUL OF FORCES REMAINING.

AND YOU HAVE A STONEKEEPER GIANT HUNTING YOU DOWN.

HUNTING US DOWN?!

NAVIN, LOOK OUT!

LANDSLIDE!

KSHOOM!!

THANKS FOR COMING TO GET US, JAIDOH.

WE CAN'T AFFORD TO LOSE YOU.

NAVIN!

MOM--

WE HAVE TO STOP DOING THIS, NAVIN.

WE CAN'T DO THIS ANYMORE.

I'M SO GLAD YOU'RE OKAY.

MOM-- I DON'T THINK THAT'S EVEN AN OPTION.

WE ARE SIMPLY OVERPOWERED. OUR POWERS ARE CRIPPLED.

LEADERSHIP... ALL THE LEADERS ARE GONE.

I HAVE SEEN A LOT OF PEOPLE MY AGE WHO HAVE THE CAPACITY TO LEAD.

MAYBE YOU JUST HAVEN'T MET THEM YET.

I KNOW THEY'RE OUT THERE.

THEY JUST NEED TO BE GIVEN A CHANCE.

IT'S TIME FOR A CHANGE, IKOL.

I KNOW WHERE YOU ARE GOING.

DON'T DO THIS, EMILY.

I HAVE WORKED HARD TO BRING THE ELVES UNDER MY COMMAND.

DO NOT ERASE THIS.

THEY ARE NOT YOUR PAWNS.

THEY CAN SENSE WHAT YOU ARE DOING, AND THAT'S WHY THEY SUFFER.

WE CAN DO BETTER.

WE CAN'T DO THE RIGHT THING THE WRONG WAY.

YOU HAVE THE POWER OF AN ENTIRE ARMY AT YOUR DISPOSAL.

DON'T THROW IT ALL AWAY.

EMILY, WAIT.

THEY FEAR YOU NOW AS THEY FEARED ME.

WILL YOU LEAD THEM?

NO.

THEY ALREADY HAVE A KING.

ZZZ.

HEY, TRELLIS.

ZZZ. SNORK!

TRELLIS!

HUH?

WE'VE ARRIVED.

CARE TO JOIN ME OUTSIDE?

OH, YES. OKAY.

WHEN MY FATHER FIRST TOLD ME ABOUT CIELIS, I THOUGHT HE WAS MAKING IT UP.

A FLYING CITY BUILT BY PEOPLE ESCAPING FROM LUCIEN, MY HOME.

THEY WERE RUNNING AWAY FROM MORE THAN JUST LUCIEN.

PERHAPS,

BUT THE LENGTHS SOME PEOPLE WILL GO TO GET AWAY FROM WHAT THEY FEAR OR DON'T UNDERSTAND--

IT'S SOMETHING I DON'T THINK I CAN EVER RELATE TO.

CAUSE ANY MORE TROUBLE AND THE RESTRAINTS GO BACK ON.

GOT IT, LOGI?

YES, PRINCE TRELLIS.

THANK YOU, PRINCE TRELLIS.

THE CIELIS GUARD WELCOMES THE RETURN OF THE GUARDIAN COUNCIL!

STONEKEEPER EMILY HAYES HAS BEEN AWAITING YOUR ARRIVAL.

EMILY'S ALREADY HERE?!

SHE IS MEETING WITH THE ARCHITECT MALORY PINE.

I UNDERSTAND THEY ARE DISCUSSING THE CREATION OF A PLAYGROUND.

A PLAYGROUND?

MISS PINE--

THIS SCHOOL IS DESIGNED LIKE YARBORO PRISON.

THE FORMER COUNCIL ASKED FOR THIS, AND I DON'T THINK THEY WERE AWARE OF THE EFFECT IT WOULD HAVE ON THE STUDENTS.

I HOPE WE CAN WORK TO IMPROVE THE SITUATION.

EMILY! YOU MADE IT BACK!

TRELLIS!

YOU LOOK HARDLY AFFECTED.

I GOT OUT FASTER THAN LUGER DID.

BUT I ALSO FEEL--

SOMETHING'S DIFFERENT.

I'M DIFFERENT.

STONEKEEPERS OF THE GUARDIAN COUNCIL.

WELCOME.

VIGO, DO YOU REMEMBER ME? I WORKED AS AN ASSISTANT FOR YOUR INSTRUCTORS AT THE ACADEMY.

YES, OF COURSE! I ALWAYS THOUGHT YOU WERE JUST ONE OF THE STUDENTS.

WE ARE THE ELDERS NOW...

YES, WE ARE.

TRELLIS, I HAVE SOMETHING TO SHOW YOU.

DOES THIS MEAN HE'S GONE?

HE WAS NEVER REALLY THERE.

IT WAS AS YOU SUSPECTED.

HE WAS BEING CONTROLLED BY THE VOICE.

JUST A GHOST.

WHAT HAPPENED TO THE VOICE?

HIS NAME IS IKOL. AND HE IS STILL WITH ME.

BUT HE WILL NO LONGER GIVE YOU TROUBLE.

AND NOW YOU HAVE THE FREEDOM TO REBUILD YOUR KINGDOM.

EMILY, WAIT.

I HAVE TO GO HELP NAVIN AND MY MOM NOW.

ON TYPHON?

BUT HOW WILL YOU GET THERE?

IT WILL TAKE DAYS TO PREPARE A SHUTTLE.

STONEKEEPERS DON'T NEED SPACESHIPS, VIGO.

I SEE.

I STILL HAVE MORE TO LEARN ABOUT OUR POWERS.

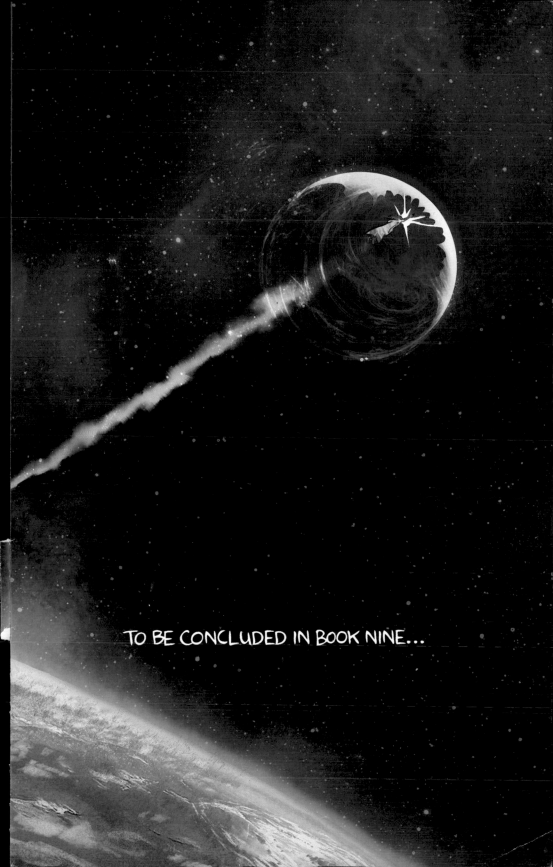

TO BE CONCLUDED IN BOOK NINE...

CREATED AT

BOLT CITY
PRODUCTIONS

WRITTEN & ILLUSTRATED BY
KAZU KIBUISHI

LEAD PRODUCTION ASSISTANT
JASON CAFFOE

COLORS & BACKGROUNDS BY
JASON CAFFOE
KAZU KIBUISHI
AMY KIM KIBUISHI
FORREST DICKISON
TIM PROBERT
POLYNA KIM
AUDRA ANN FURUICHI
DERICK TSAI
AMANDA JANE SHARPE
JOE MARQUIS
KELLY HAMILTON

PAGE FLATTING
CRYSTAL KAN
MEGAN BRENNAN
POLYNA KIM
JOEY HAN
AUDRA ANN FURUICHI
LINDSEY REIMER
PRESTON DO

SPECIAL THANKS
Judith Hansen, Cassandra Pelham Fulton, Phil Falco, David Saylor,
Nancy Caffoe, Juni & Sophie Kibuishi, Rachel & Hazel Caffoe,
Dan & Heidi Ullom, Moses Phillips, Bart Foutch, and Ryan Brown
and the Bicycle Centres crew.

Thank you to all the librarians, booksellers, parents, and readers
for whom this book was made.

About the Author

Kazu Kibuishi is the creator of the #1 *New York Times* bestselling Amulet series, which is available in 16 languages. *Amulet, Book One: The Stonekeeper* was an ALA Best Book for Young Adults and a Children's Choice Book Award finalist. He is also the creator of *Copper*, a collection of his popular webcomic that features an adventuresome boy-and-dog pair. Kazu also illustrated the covers of the 15th anniversary paperback editions of the Harry Potter series written by J.K. Rowling. He lives and works near Seattle, Washington, with his wife, Amy Kim Kibuishi, and their children.

Visit Kazu online at www.boltcity.com.

WINDSOR

Ice Prison of Korthan

Gondoa Mountain

TAKA RIVER

NOBUO RANGE

Kanalis

Demon's Head Mountain

Black Forest

Gorbon

Nautilus

Drucker Canyon

COCONINO MOUNTAINS

COCONINO VALLEY

Pomo

LUFEN